Gg Hh Ii Jj Kk Ll Mm

Uu Vv Ww Xx Yy Zz

Dear Parent,

The My First Steps to Reading® series is based on a teaching activity that helps children learn to recognize letters and their sounds. The use of predictable language patterns and repetition of familiar words will also help your child build a basic sight vocabulary. Your child will enjoy watching the characters in the books place imaginative objects in "letter boxes." You and your child can even create and fill your own letter box, using stuffed animals, cut-out pictures, or other objects beginning with the same letter. The things you can do together are limited only by your imagination. Learning letters will be fun—the first important step on the road to reading.

The Editors

My "j" Book

written by Jane Belk Moncure

illustrated by Colin King

Little  had a box.

"I will find things that begin with my 'j' sound," he said.

"I will put them into

my sound  box."

But first, Little 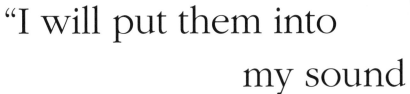 put on

his jeans and jacket.

"I will jump," he said.

He jumped over the box
like a jumping jack.

Then he jumped  into the box.

"I am a jack-in-the-box!" he said.
He jumped up.

Little jumped up a hill.

"I will jump like Jack and Jill," he said.

He jumped down the hill.
Then he saw a . . .

 jack-o'-lantern.

Did he put the
jack-o'-lantern into
his box? He did.

Then Little J jumped until he saw . . .

jackrabbits!

He saw lots of jumping jackrabbits.

Did he put the jumping jackrabbits into the box with the jack-o'-lantern? He did.

Then he jumped until he saw . . .

jays.

The jays cried, *"jay, jay, jay!"*

Little  put them into the box with the jack-o'-lantern and the jackrabbits.

Now the box was full, so . . .

Little  found a jeep.

He put the box with the jackrabbits,
jays, and jack-o'-lantern into the jeep . . .

and drove into the jungle.

Just then, Little

saw a   jaguar.

The jaguar was about to jump
on the jackrabbits!

Little held up the
jack-o'-lantern and . . .

the jaguar jumped away!

Little  caught the jaguar.

He took him
to jail

so he could not jump on the jackrabbits.

Just then,

Little saw Jumbo,

the jolly elephant.

"Jumbo is too big for my sound box," he said.

Little  found a jet. A jumbo jet!
It was big enough for the
animals and everything else.

Jumbo

jackrabbits

jumbo jet

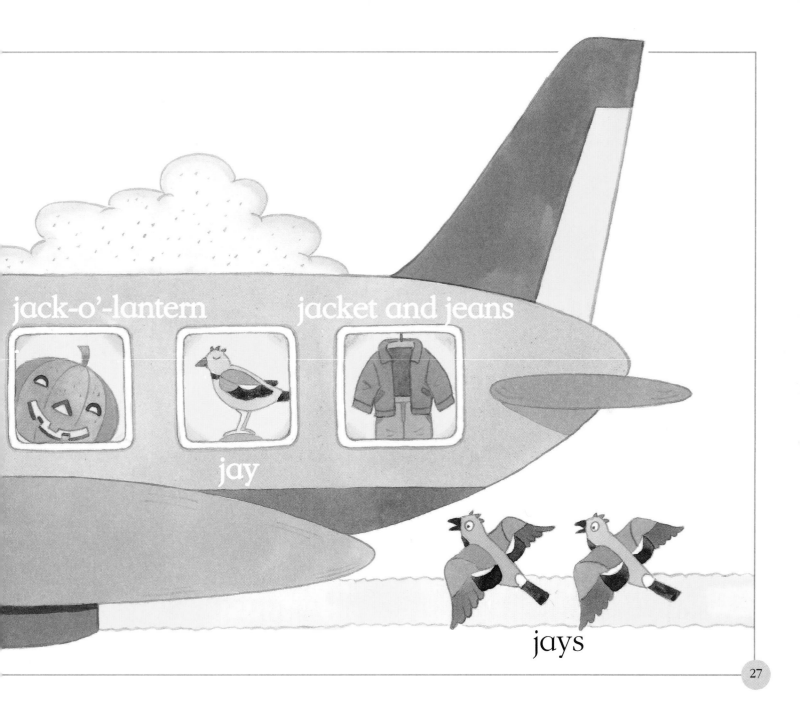

jack-o'-lantern

jacket and jeans

jay

jays

27

Can you read these words with Little J?

jar

jonquil

jacks

jewels

jackal

jellyfish

January

1	2	3	4	5	6	7
8	9	10	11	12	13	14
15	16	17	18	19	20	21
22	23	24	25	26	27	28
29	30	31				

June

				1	2	3
4	5	6	7	8	9	10
11	12	13	14	15	16	17
18	19	20	21	22	23	24
25	26	27	28	29	30	

July

			1	2	3	4
5	6	7	8	9	10	11
12	13	14	15	16	17	18
19	20	21	22	23	24	25
26	27	28	29	30	31	

juggler

juice

Aa Bb Cc Dd Ee Ff

Nn Oo Pp Qq Rr Ss Tt

My First Steps to READING®